NICK JR
Blue's Clues®

My Favorite Letters

by Deborah Reber
illustrated by Karen Craig

Ready-to-I

Simon Spotlight/ Nick Jr.

New York   London   Toronto   Sydney   Singapore

To Alice Wilder . . . I'm so glad you're my friend!—D. R.
For Grammy, PopPop, Nanna, and—of course—Dadooooo!—K.C.

Based on the TV series *Blue's Clues*® created by Traci Paige Johnson, Todd Kessler, and Angela C. Santomero as seen on Nick Jr.®
On *Blue's Clues* Steve is played by Steven Burns.

SIMON SPOTLIGHT
An imprint of Simon & Schuster Children's Publishing Division
1230 Avenue of the Americas, New York, New York 10020
Copyright © 2001 Viacom International Inc.
10   Manufactured in the United States of America
ISBN 0-689-83797-6

Library of Congress Cataloging-in-Publication Data

Reber, Deborah
        My favorite letters / by Deborah Reber ; illustrated by Karen Craig.
            p. cm. — (Ready-to-read)
        "Based on the TV series Blues Clues"—T.p. verso.
        Summary: Blue learns to spell her name and finds other words that begin
with her favorite letters: B, L, U, and E. Features rebuses.
        ISBN 0-689-83797-6
        1. Rebuses. [1. Dogs—Fiction. 2. Vocabulary—Fiction. 3. Rebuses.] I. Craig,
Karen S.,
        ill. II. Title. III. Series.

    PZ7.R23775 My 2001
    [E]—dc21
    00-041948

Hi, I am  BLUE ! I just learned to spell my name at SCHOOL.

B-L-U-E! They are my 4 favorite

FOUR

letters in the whole alphabet!

Look, I wrote my name in the  SAND TABLE with a ___. STICK Can you see? Even the ☁️ CLOUDS are spelling my name!

The  in the

FLOWERS

 can spell my

GARDEN

name, too.

What great letters!
And they start so
many great words.

B begins my name,
and it begins lots
of words in this
picture I made. It is
called "'s  in
BLUE   BUBBLES
the ."
BATHTUB

Here is the  that

BOOK

BABY BEAR got me for my

birthday!

MR. SALT and MRS. PEPPER are baking

BANANA BREAD for Steve.

Baking BANANA BREAD . All of those words start with B!

And look!

Here is something that starts with L: for my to

LEMONADE   LUNCHBOX

take with me to 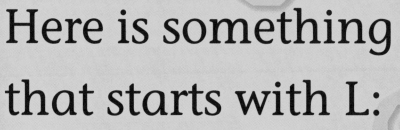!

SCHOOL

Here is a  from

LETTER

 that makes me

MAGENTA

laugh out loud!

, laugh, and

LETTER

loud all start with

L too!

What about U? I like that letter, too. It is the first letter of  .

UMBRELLA

And U is the first letter of  . Do you like U? Me too!

UNDERWEAR

And then there is E.
E is the first letter
for , elbows,
EARS
and !
EYES
I can build an E
with ice cream
STICKS
and .
GLUE

Or, I can paint the  on my .

EARTH

EASEL

E is the first letter of . They go inside

ENVELOPES

. Look! has

MAILBOX   MAILBOX

a 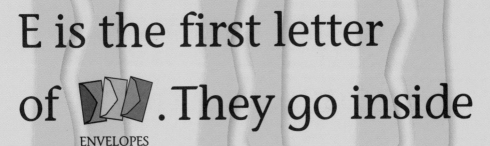 for me!

LETTER

How do I know?
Because my name
is right here. B-L-U-E.
Blue!